THE CAT CAME BACK

Kids Can Press Ltd. acknowledges with appreciation the assistance of the Canada Council and the Ontario Arts Council in the production of this book.

CANADIAN CATALOGUING IN PUBLICATION DATA
Main entry under title:

The Cat came back

Unacc. melody.
ISBN 1-55074-071-7

1. Children's songs.   I. Slavin, Bill.

M1998.C3 1992   j782′.42   C91-095406-2

Kids Can Press Ltd.,
585½ Bloor Street West,
Toronto, Ontario, Canada, M6G 1K5.

Printed and bound in Hong Kong

92 0 9 8 7 6 5 4 3 2 1

For my brother Jim,
who knows all the words.

THE CAT

A traditional song
illustrated by Bill Slavin

KIDS CAN PRESS LTD.
Toronto

CAME BACK

Old Mister Johnson had
troubles of his own,
He had a yellow cat that
wouldn't leave his home.

He tried and he tried
to give that cat away,

He found an ocean liner going far, far away.

But the cat came back
    the very next day,
The cat came back,
    they thought he was a goner,
The cat came back,
    he just wouldn't stay away.

Mister Johnson gave the cat
to a man in a balloon,
He said, "Please take this cat
and leave it on the moon."

The balloon came down about
ninety miles away,
Where the man is now, well,
no one wants to say.

And the cat came back
    the very next day,
The cat came back,
    they thought he was a goner,
The cat came back,
    he just wouldn't stay away.

Mister Johnson gave the cat to a fellow heading west,

He said, "The cat's a present for the one you love the best."

First the train hit the track, then it bounced and jumped a rail,

Not a person stayed around to tell the gruesome tale.

And the cat came back
   the very next day,
The cat came back,
   they thought he was a goner,
The cat came back,
   he just wouldn't stay away.

The cat was now the father of a family of his own,
They lived with Mister Johnson 'til there came a cyclone.

It tore the house apart and tossed the cats around,
The air was filled with kittens,

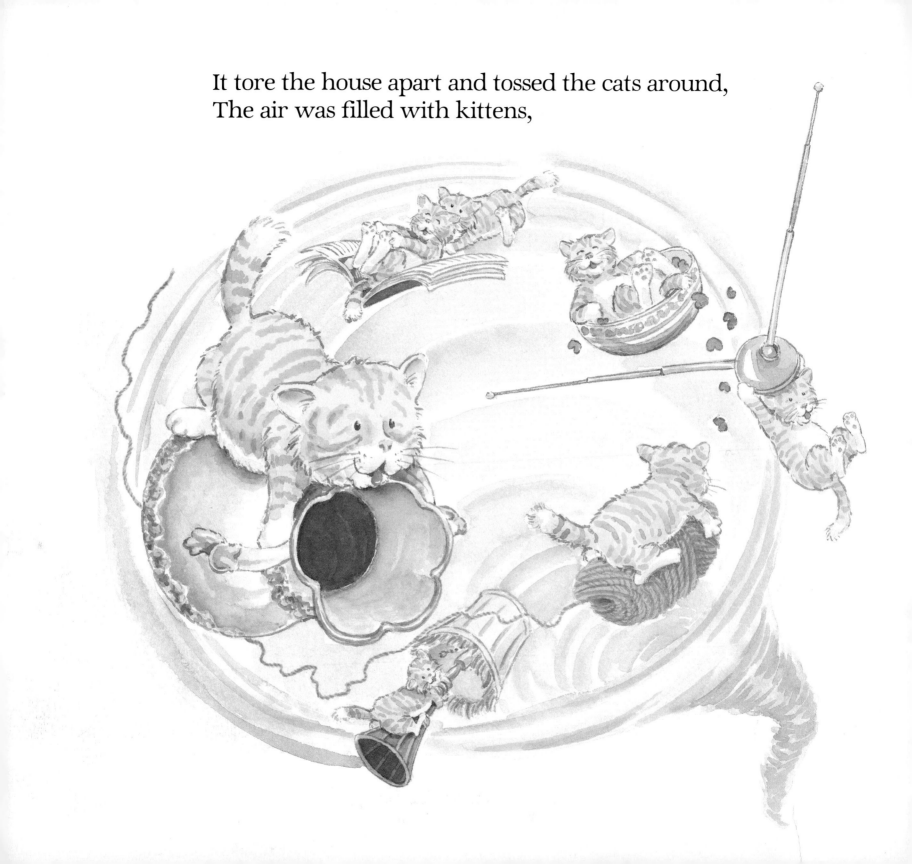

the cat could not be found.

But the cat came back
  the very next day,
The cat came back,
  they thought he was a goner,
The cat came back,
  he just wouldn't stay away.

THE CAT CAME BACK

Old   Mis- ter   John-son   had   trou- bles   of   his   own, He

had   a   yel- low   cat   that   would- n't   leave   his   home. He

tried   and   he   tried   to   give   that   cat   a- way. He

found an   o- cean   lin- er   go- ing   far,   far   a-way. But the